coming and going

Tate Publishing

The head, it is said, is not just for wearing a hat.
Feet, we might also say, are not just for wearing shoes.
We use our legs and feet to walk, run, come and go.

We move just like the Earth moves.

A long time ago, we walked slowly for days on end, looking for food or some shelter for the night.

Sometimes we ran as fast as our legs could carry us.

Then we rode horses,
we invented wheels and carts,
cars, trains and boats,
planes and rockets.

We sat at the wheel feeling very pleased
with ourselves.
And in no time at all we were covering
longer distances than ever before.

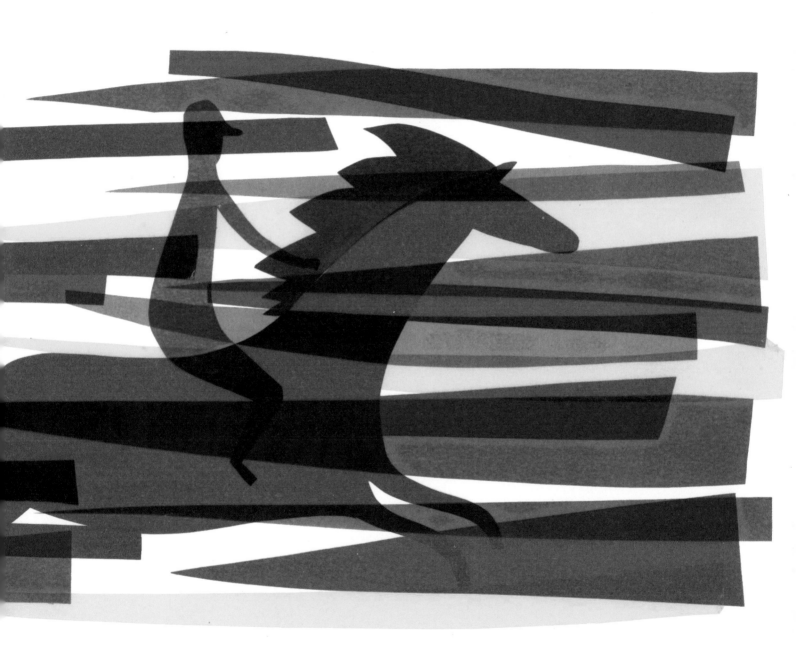

This set us humans apart as a special kind of animal.
(Not to be compared with zebras, birds or butterflies.)
We were the true champions of space.
Distance, at least on Earth, was child's play.

We grew used to coming and going.
To fetching and carrying
things and people, children, adults,
grannies and babies, packets and parcels,
large and small.

Cruising along
or with our foot to the pedal,
we could now carry
everything around town:
clothes, shoes, timber, pears,
cars, flour, clocks, chairs,
mangoes, bananas, garlic and biscuits
flowers and computers...

and little rubber ducks.

Everything coming and going,
easily enough,
here and there.

But what does 'easily' mean?

'Easily' is easy to say...
We had to open new roads,
dig through mountains,
build railways and roads.
We had to take great leaps.

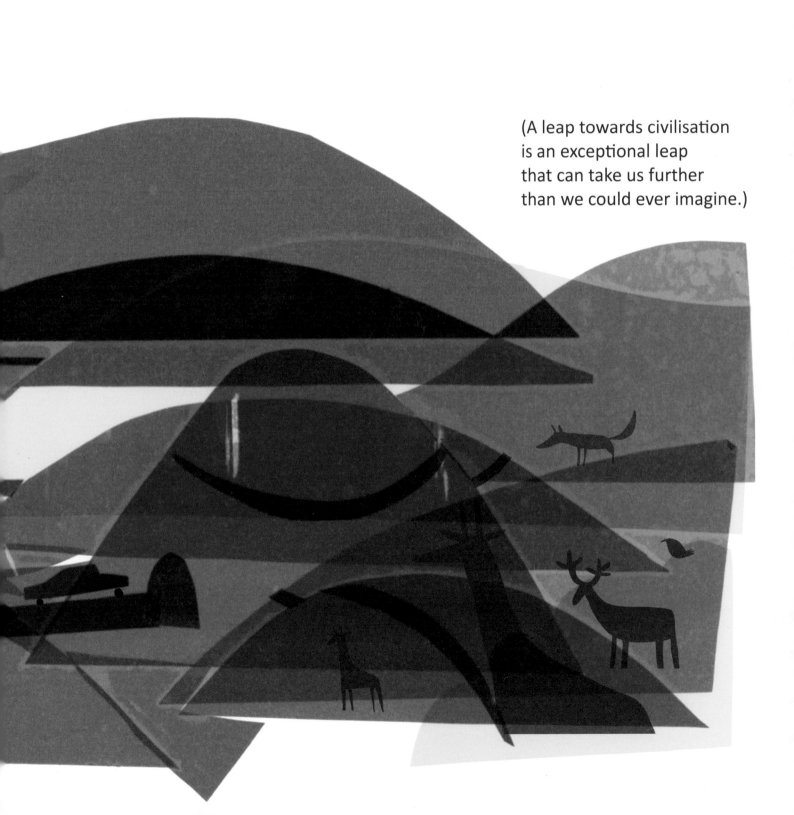

(A leap towards civilisation
is an exceptional leap
that can take us further
than we could ever imagine.)

But because great feats are what we're best at,
we took not one leap but many,
without looking back.
And so we became champions.
A round of applause for us!
Forging ahead day after day!
From other animals ever further away.

In our eagerness, we wanted to go supersonic.
In our eagerness, we hunted for super fuels.
In our eagerness, we almost blew the fuses...
(no, not ours, but the planet's).

If we knew more about the movements
of other animals, perhaps we'd blush.

Just look at the Arctic tern.
Take in all its beauty...

Every year, this little bird crosses the globe in search of warmer lands.

For a tern, it's summer wherever he goes.

As far as we know, terns don't have engines
(just a tiny heart) and yet, in just one year,
they can travel 50,000 miles,
without bothering a soul.

Monarch butterflies are no less spectacular.
When the days begin to get shorter,
they head south, flying thousands of miles.

The life span of a butterfly is short,
so several generations come and go along the way.

But the group never forgets its destination
and the butterflies that reach it are the
grandchildren or the great-great-grandchildren
of those that first set out
(and true heroines at that!).

Imagine: millions of butterflies, flying and flying for months on end and never filling up the tank.

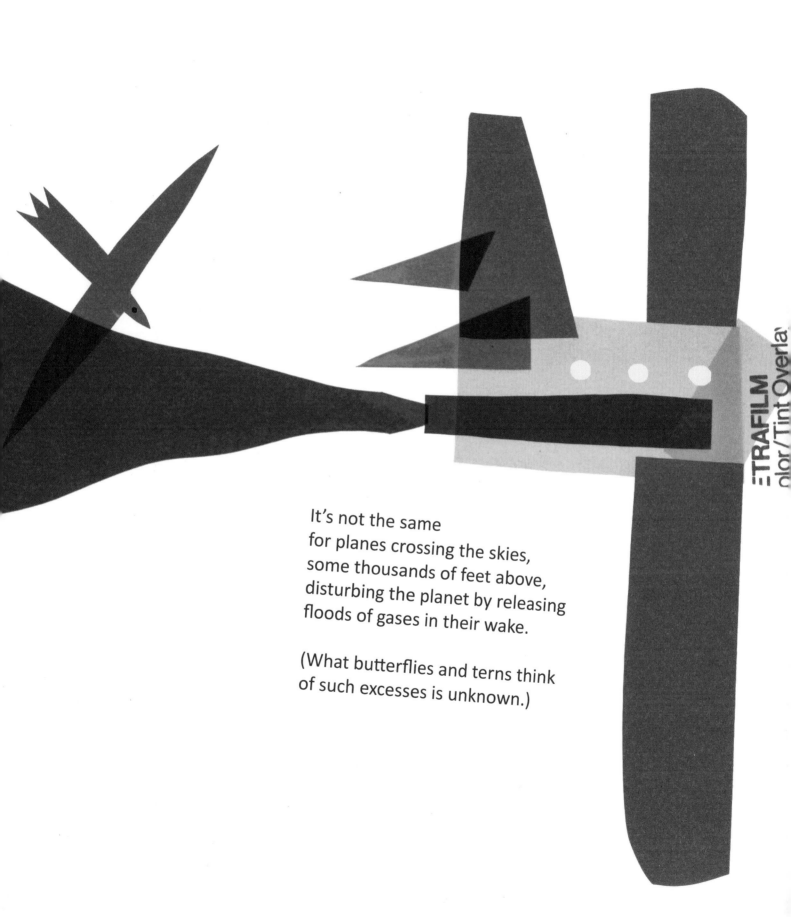

It's not the same
for planes crossing the skies,
some thousands of feet above,
disturbing the planet by releasing
floods of gases in their wake.

(What butterflies and terns think
of such excesses is unknown.)

And take the baleen whale, for example.
Despite its 36,000 kilograms
(it weighs more than two buses!)
every year it travels some 6,500 miles
to have its young.

The most impressive thing is that it does so discreetly and full of grace.
Almost without bothering a soul...

Tuna travel for the same reasons
but they're much faster than whales.

This school we see here
swims at 40 miles per hour,
completely unaware that a few yards ahead,
a freighter carrying cans of tuna
is tearing across the water.

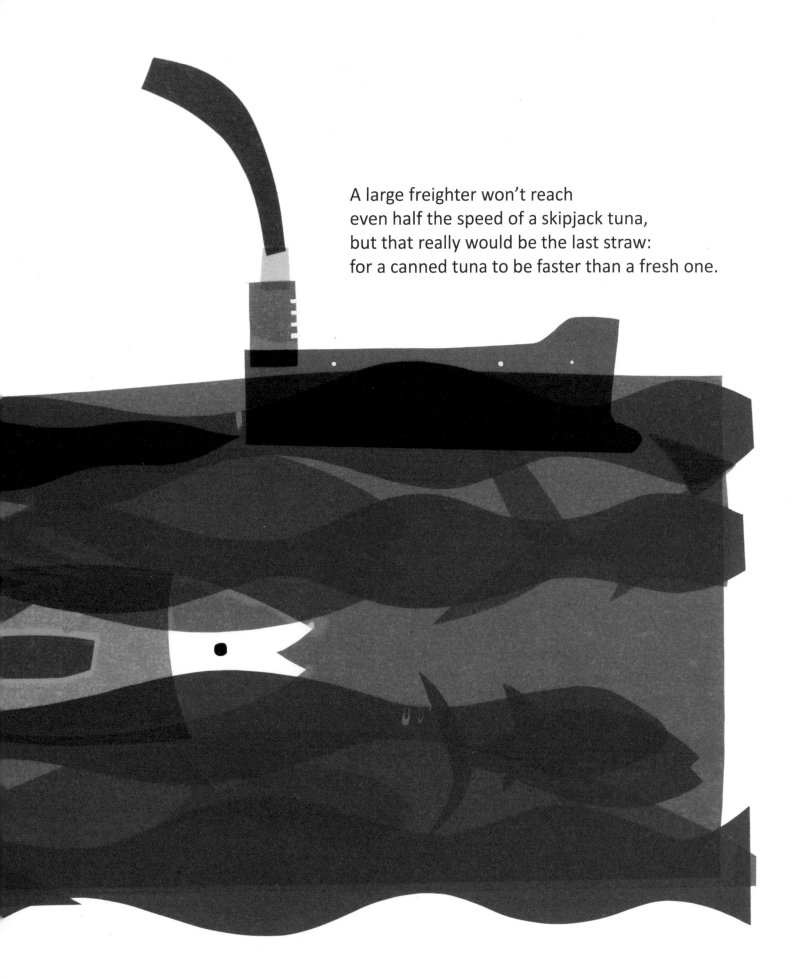

A large freighter won't reach
even half the speed of a skipjack tuna,
but that really would be the last straw:
for a canned tuna to be faster than a fresh one.

There are also incredible travellers on land. Wildebeest, for example, move a long way north in the dry season in search of green pastures and cool water.

Zebras join them on this journey and often they're not the only ones.

Predators, including man, do so too.

A wildebeest can reach speeds of 40 miles per hour.
A jeep, as long as it doesn't run out of fuel, can go a lot faster.
Yet a jeep is not a wildebeest… whenever it revs, smoke billows
into the sky (where butterflies and terns peacefully fly).

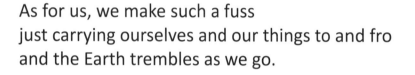

Turtles, albatrosses, salmon, shearwaters,
elephant seals, sharks and even lobsters
travel around the Earth without upsetting its balance.

As for us, we make such a fuss
just carrying ourselves and our things to and fro
and the Earth trembles as we go.

Perhaps it would do good to remember
that our feet are not just for wearing shoes
and our head is not just for wearing a hat.

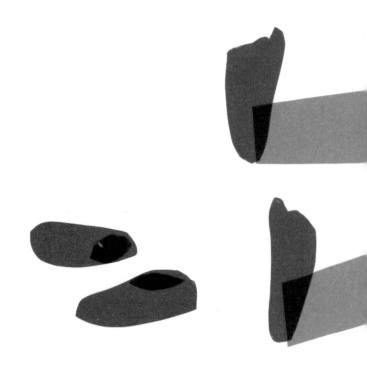

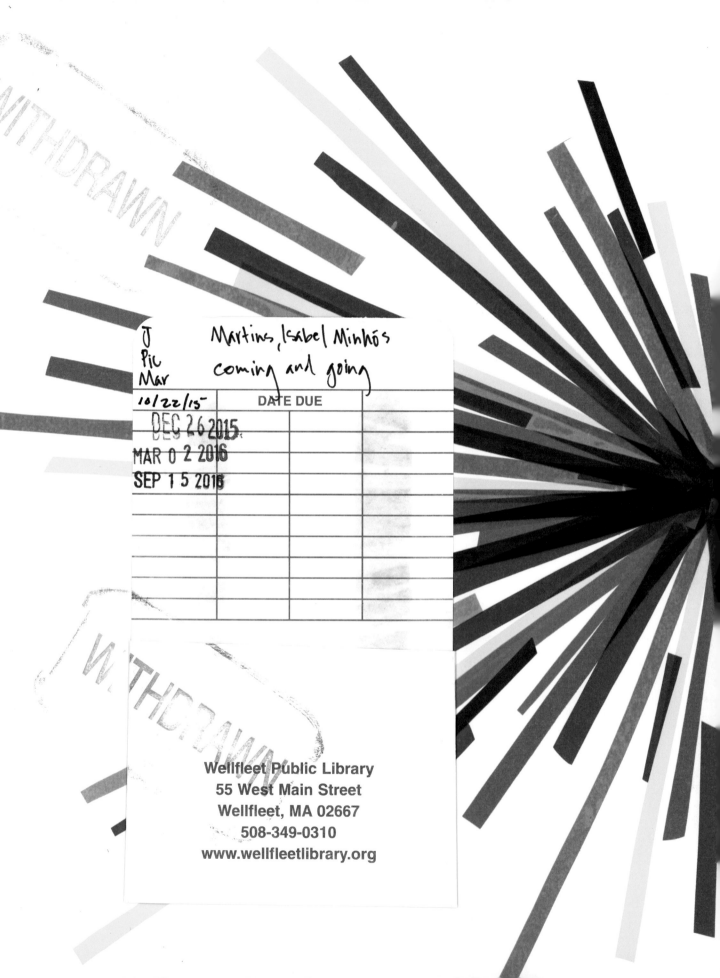